The
BEAR
THAT
WASN'T

The

BEAR
THAT
WASN'T

By

FRANK
TASHLIN

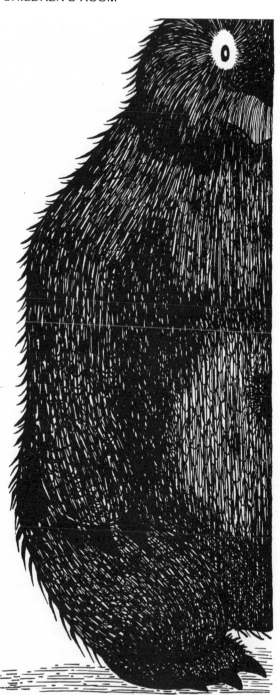

NEW YORK
THE NEW YORK REVIEW CHILDREN'S COLLECTION

THIS IS A NEW YORK REVIEW BOOK
PUBLISHED BY THE NEW YORK REVIEW OF BOOKS

First published by E. P. Dutton & Co., 1946

Published in the United States of America by
New York Review Books, 435 Hudson Street, New York, NY 10014
www.nyrb.com

Library of Congress Cataloging-in-Publication Data

Tashlin, Frank.
The bear that wasn't / by Frank Tashlin.
p. cm. — (New York Review Books children's collection)
Summary: After hibernating for the winter, a bear wakes up to discover that a
huge factory has been built over his cave and that nobody believes he is a bear.
ISBN 978-1-59017-344-2 (alk. paper)
[1. Bears—Fiction. 2. Identity—Fiction.] I. Title. II. Title: Bear that was not.
PZ7.T21114Be 2010
[Fic]—dc22
2009031683

ISBN 978-1-59017-344-2

Cover design by Louise Fili Ltd.

Printed in the United States on acid-free paper.
3 5 7 9 10 8 6 4 2

TO

PATRICIA ANNE

THE

LITTLE

GIRL

THAT

IS.

Once upon a time, in fact it was on a Tuesday, the Bear stood at the edge of a great forest and gazed up at the sky. Away up high, he saw a flock of geese flying south.

Then he gazed up at the trees of the forest. The leaves
had turned all yellow and brown and were falling
from the branches.

He knew when the geese flew south and the leaves fell
from the trees, that winter would soon be here and snow
would cover the forest. It was time to go into a cave
and hibernate.

And that was just what he did.

Not long afterward, in fact it was on a Wednesday, men came . . . lots of men, with charts and maps and surveying instruments. They charted and mapped and surveyed all over the place.

Then more men came, lots of men with steamshovels and
saws and tractors and axes. They steamshoveled and
sawed and tractored and axed all over the place.

They worked, and worked, and worked, and finally they
built a great, big, huge,

factory, right **OVER** the **TOP** of the sleeping Bear's cave.

The factory operated all through the cold winter.

And

then

it

was

SPRING

again

Deep down under one of the factory
buildings the Bear awoke. He
blinked his eyes and yawned.

Then he stood up sleepily and
looked around. It was very dark. He
could hardly see.

Then he saw a light in the distance.
"Oh, there's the entrance to the cave,"
he said, and yawned again.

He walked up the stairs to the
entrance

and stepped out into the bright
spring sunshine. His eyes were
only half opened, as he was still
very sleepy.

His eyes didn't stay half opened
long.

They suddenly POPPED
wide apart.
He looked straight ahead.

Where was the forest?
Where was the grass?
Where were the trees?
Where were the flowers?

WHAT HAD HAPPENED?

Where was he?

Things looked so strange. He didn't know
where he was.

But we do, don't we? We know that he was right in the
middle of the busy factory.

"I must be dreaming," he said.
"Of course that's it, I'm dreaming." So he
closed his eyes and pinched himself.
Then he opened his eyes very
slowly and looked about. The big
buildings were still there. It wasn't
a dream. It was real.

Just then a man came out of
a door.

"Hey, you get back to work,"
the man said. "I'm the
Foreman and I'll report you
for not working."

The Bear said, "I don't
work here. I'm a Bear."

The Foreman laughed very loud.

"That's a fine excuse for a man to keep
from doing any work."

"Saying he's a Bear."

The Bear said, "But, I am a Bear."

The Foreman stopped laughing. He was very mad.

"Don't try to fool me," he said. "You're not a Bear. You're a silly man who needs a shave and wears a fur coat. I'm going to take you to the *General Manager*."

The Bear said, "No, you're mistaken. I am a Bear."

The General Manager was very mad, too.

He said, "You're not a Bear. You're a silly man who needs a shave and wears a fur coat. I'm going to take you to the *Third* Vice President."

The Bear said, "I'm sorry to hear you say that . . . You see, I am a Bear."

The Third Vice President was
even madder.

He got up out of his chair and said,
"You're not a Bear. You're a silly
man who needs a shave and wears
a fur coat. I'm going to take you
to the *Second* Vice President."

The Bear leaned over his desk and
said, "But that isn't true. I am
a Bear, just a plain, ordinary,
everyday Bear."

The Second Vice President was more than mad or madder. He was furious.

He pointed his finger at the Bear and said, "You're not a Bear. You're a silly man who needs a shave and wears a fur coat. I'm going to take you to the *First* Vice President."

"Who? Me?" the Bear asked. "How can you say that, when I am a Bear?"

The First Vice President yelled in rage.

He said, "You're not a Bear. You're a silly man who needs a shave and wears a fur coat. I'm going to take you to the *President*."

The Bear pleaded, "This is a dreadful error, you know, because ever since I can remember, I've always been a Bear."

"Listen," the Bear told the President, "I don't work here.
I'm a Bear, and please don't say I'm a silly man who needs
a shave and wears a fur coat, because the
First Vice President and the Second Vice President
and the Third Vice President and the General Manager

and the Foreman, have told me that already."

"Thank you for telling me," the President said. "I won't say it, but that's just what I think you are."

The Bear said, "I'm a Bear."

The President smiled and said,
"You can't be a Bear. Bears are only
in a zoo or a circus. They're never
inside a factory and that's where
you are; inside a factory. So how
can you be a Bear?"

The Bear said, "But I am a Bear."

The President said, "Not only are you a silly man who **needs** a shave and wears **a fur** coat, but **you are** also very stubborn. So I'm going **to prove** it to you, once and for all, that you are *not* a Bear."

The Bear said, "But I *am* a Bear."

AND

SO

THEY

ALL

GOT

INTO

THE

PRESIDENT'S

CAR

AND

DROVE

TO

THE

ZOO

DO NOT
FEED THE
ANIMALS

ZOO

"Is he a *Bear?*" the President asked the zoo Bears.

The zoo Bears said, "No, he isn't a Bear, because if he were a Bear, he wouldn't be outside the cage with you. He would be inside the cage with us."

The Bear said, "But I am a Bear."

A little baby zoo Bear said, "I know what he is. He's a silly man who needs a shave and wears a fur coat."

All the zoo Bears laughed.

The Bear said, "But I am a Bear."

AND

SO

THEY

ALL

LEFT

THE

ZOO

AND

DROVE

SIX

HUNDRED

MILES

AWAY

TO

THE

NEAREST

CIRCUS

"Is he a *Bear?*" the President asked the circus Bears.

The circus Bears said, "No, he isn't a Bear, because if ne were a Bear, he wouldn't be sitting in a grandstand seat with you. He would be wearing a little hat with a striped ribbon on it, holding on to a balloon and riding a bicycle with us." The Bear said, "But I am a Bear."

One little baby circus Bear said, "I know what he is. He's
a silly man who needs a shave and wears a fur coat."

All the circus Bears almost fell off their bicycles laughing.

The Bear said, "But I am a Bear."

They left the circus and drove
back to the factory.

And so they put the Bear to work on a big machine with a lot of other men. The Bear worked on the big machine for many, many months.

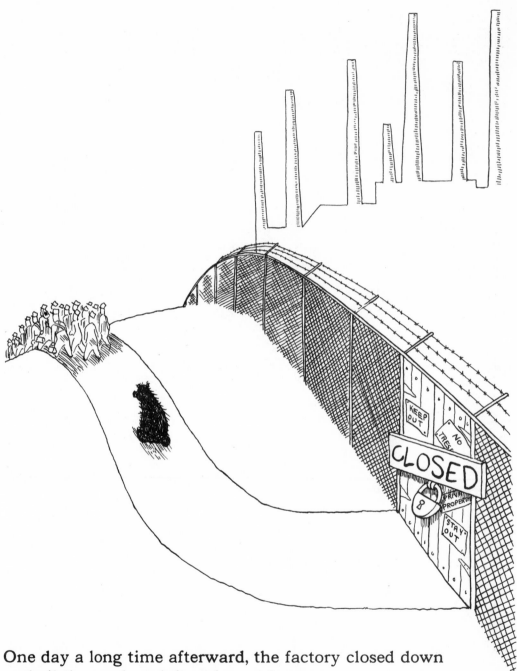

One day a long time afterward, the factory closed down
and all the workers left and went home.
The Bear walked along far behind them. He was all
alone, and had no place to go.

As he walked along, he happened to gaze up at the sky. Away up high, he saw a flock of geese flying south.

Then the Bear gazed up at the trees. The leaves had turned all yellow and brown and were falling from the branches.

The Bear knew when the geese flew south and the leaves
fell from the trees, that winter would soon be here and
snow would cover the forest. It was time to go into a
cave and hibernate.

So he walked over to a huge tree that had a cave hollowed
out beneath its roots. He was just about to go into it,
when he stopped and said,

"But I **CAN'T** go into a cave and hibernate.
I'm **NOT** a Bear. I'm a silly man who needs a shave
and wears a fur coat."

So winter came. The snow fell. It covered the forest and it covered him. He sat there, shivering with cold and he said, "But I sure wish I was a Bear."

The longer he sat there the colder he became. His toes were freezing, his ears were freezing and his teeth were chattering. Icicles covered his nose and chin. He had been told so often, that he was a silly man who needed a shave and wore a fur coat, that he felt it must be true.

So he just sat there, because he didn't know what a silly man who needed a shave and wore a fur coat would do, if he were freezing to death in the snow. The poor Bear was very lonely and very sad. He didn't know what to think.

Then suddenly he got up and walked through the deep snow toward the cave.

Inside, it was cosy and snug. The icy wind and cold, cold snow couldn't reach him here. He felt warm all over.

He sank down on a bed of pine boughs and soon he was happily asleep and dreaming sweet dreams, just like all bears do, when they hibernate.

So even though the

FOREMAN
and the
GENERAL MANAGER
and the
THIRD VICE-PRESIDENT
and the
SECOND VICE-PRESIDENT

and the
FIRST VICE-PRESIDENT
and the
PRESIDENT
and the
ZOO BEARS
and the
CIRCUS BEARS

had said, he was a silly man who **needed** a shave and wore **a fur** coat, I don't think he really believed it, do you? No, indeed, he knew **he wasn't** a silly man,

and he **wasn't** a silly Bear either.

FRANK TASHLIN (1913–1972) was born in New Jersey and raised in Queens, New York. As a teenager he worked as an errand boy, inker, and animator at several pioneering animation studios in New York. By 1933 he had moved to Hollywood, where he wrote and directed cartoon shorts for MGM and Warner Bros., and briefly served as head of production at Screen Gems. Tashlin also worked for a while at Disney Studios, helping to organize its embattled animators' union. During his early years in California, Tashlin drew a syndicated pantomime-style cartoon strip called *Van Boring*, and during the Second World War, he worked on the military's Private Snafu series (created by Frank Capra and Theodor "Dr. Seuss" Geisel). Though he retired from animation in the mid-1940s, Tashlin is recognized as an influential stylist who brought cinematographic techniques and inventive "camera" angles to the medium. Moving from cartoons to live action, Tashlin worked for a time as a comedy writer before fulfilling his ambition to write and direct feature films. He is best known for his collaborations with Jerry Lewis and Bob Hope, and for screwball comedies like *The Girl Can't Help It* and *Will Success Spoil Rock Hunter?* Tashlin has described *The Bear That Wasn't* (1946) as "precious and special to me." It was followed by two more picture books, *The 'Possum That Didn't* (1950) and *The World That Wasn't* (1951).

PENELOPE FARMER
Charlotte Sometimes

RUMER GODDEN
An Episode of Sparrows
The Mousewife

LUCRETIA P. HALE
The Peterkin Papers

RUSSELL and LILLIAN HOBAN
The Sorely Trying Day

RUTH KRAUSS and MARC SIMONT
The Backward Day

MUNRO LEAF and ROBERT LAWSON
Wee Gillis

NORMAN LINDSAY
The Magic Pudding

ERIC LINKLATER
The Wind on the Moon

J. P. MARTIN
Uncle
Uncle Cleans Up

JOHN MASEFIELD
The Midnight Folk
The Box of Delights

E. NESBIT
The House of Arden

BARBARA SLEIGH
Carbonel: The King of the Cats
The Kingdom of Carbonel
Carbonel and Calidor

FRANK TASHLIN
The Bear That Wasn't

JAMES THURBER
The 13 Clocks
The Wonderful O

T. H. WHITE
Mistress Masham's Repose

REINER ZIMNIK
The Bear and the People
The Crane